Chapter

Ricky Ricotta's Mighty Robot vs the Mecha-Monkeys from Mars

The Fourth Robot Adventure Novel by

DAV PILKEY

Pictures by

MARTIN ONTIVEROS

For Felix
— D. P.

To Felix Salvador Ontiveros:
I can't wait to read this one to you!
— M. O.

Scholastic Children's Books,
Euston House, 24 Eversholt Street,
London, NW 1 1DB, UK
a division of Scholastic Ltd
London ~ New York ~ Toronto ~ Sydney ~ Auckland
Mexico City ~ New Delhi ~ Hong Kong

First published in the US by Scholastic Inc., 2001

First published in the UK by Scholastic Ltd, 2002

Text copyright © Dav Pilkey, 2001
Illustrations copyright © Martin Ontiveros, 2001

10 digit ISBN 0 439 97942 0
13 digit ISBN 978 0439 97942 9

Printed and bound in Denmark by Nørhaven Paperback A/S, Viborg

6 8 10 9 7

CHAPTER 1

The Big Mistake

One day, Ricky Ricotta
and his mighty Robot were
playing hide and seek
in their garden.

"This game is too easy," said
Ricky. "Let's ride skateboards
instead!"

Ricky got his skateboard out of the
garage, but there was no skateboard
big enough for his mighty Robot.

"I know," said Ricky. "We can use my parents' people carrier!"

Soon, Ricky and his mighty Robot
were zooming down the street.
"This is fun!" said Ricky.

But it stopped being fun
when they fell over.
CRASH!

When Ricky and his Robot
got out of the pond, they saw the
smashed-up people carrier.

"Uh-oh," said Ricky.
"We're in big trouble now!"

Ricky's mighty Robot put the
people carrier back in the driveway.

"Maybe Mum and Dad won't
notice," said Ricky.

16

But they did.

CHAPTER 2

Big Trouble

Ricky's mother and father were
not happy.

"All right," said Ricky's father.
"Which one of you boys squished
our people carrier?"

Ricky and his mighty Robot
looked down at the ground.
They were very worried.

Finally, Ricky confessed.
"We both did," said Ricky.
"It was an accident."

"You boys were very irresponsible," said Ricky's father.

"Yes," said Ricky's mother, "and you will have to find a way to pay for the damage you have done."

CHAPTER 3

Major Monkey Hates Mars

Meanwhile, about 56 million kilometres away on the planet Mars, there lived a mean little monkey who was hatching an evil plan.

His name was Major Monkey,
and he hated living on Mars.
Mars was a cold, dry and
very, very lonely place.

Major Monkey kept himself busy by building evil Robots and strange machines in his secret laboratory, but he was still lonely.

There was nobody to talk to. There was nobody to yell at . . . and, worst of all, there was nobody to be mean to.

So Major Monkey decided to take over the planet Earth and enslave all of mousekind.

Major Monkey had watched Earth for many months. He saw other evil villains try to take over the planet, but they were always stopped by Ricky Ricotta's mighty Robot.

BANANA JUICE

"I must get rid of that mighty
Robot!" said Major Monkey.
"And I know just how to do it."

CHAPTER 4

The Trap

The next morning, as Ricky and his mighty Robot walked to school, they tried to think of a way to pay for their mistake of wrecking the people carrier.

"How many years will it take to buy a new people carrier with my pocket money?" asked Ricky.

Ricky's Robot used his super brain to figure out the answer. "Hmmm," said Ricky. "Only 259 years? Maybe we should think of a better plan."

Suddenly, a small spaceship
zoomed out of the sky. The top
of the spaceship opened up,
and a spacemouse peeked out.

31

"Help us! Help us!" cried the spacemouse. "Mars is under attack! We need your mighty Robot to save us!"

Ricky Ricotta's mighty Robot could not turn away from someone who needed help. So the mighty Robot followed the tiny spaceship all the way to Mars.

"Be careful up there!"
Ricky shouted.

CHAPTER 5

Betrayed

Ricky's mighty Robot soon arrived
on Mars. He saw a strange laboratory,
but he did not see any
evil villains.

The mighty Robot flew closer to the laboratory. Suddenly, a giant metal hand reached out of the hillside.

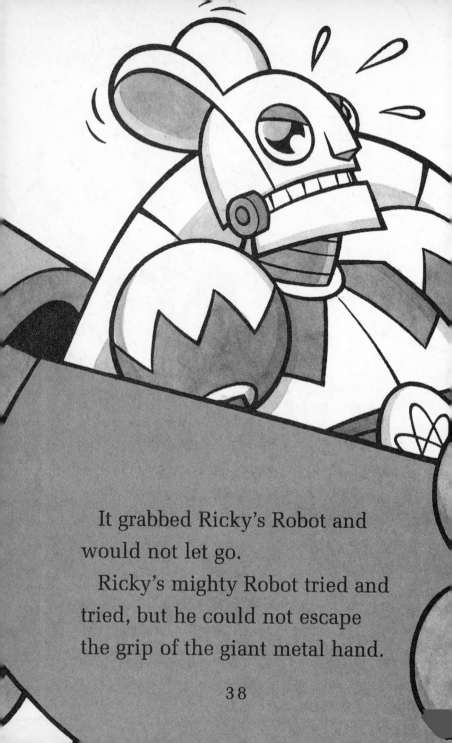

It grabbed Ricky's Robot and would not let go.

Ricky's mighty Robot tried and tried, but he could not escape the grip of the giant metal hand.

Major Monkey looked up from
the tiny spaceship and pulled
a puppet off his hand.

"I tricked you! I tricked you!"
Major Monkey mocked. "Now
it is YOU who needs help!
Haw-haw-haw!"

Major Monkey pressed a button inside his spaceship. Soon, three giant Mecha-Monkeys rose from the depths of the strange laboratory.

Major Monkey called out to his troops: "Mecha-Monkeys!" he cried. "It is time to take over Earth. Follow ME!"

CHAPTER 6

Major Monkey Makes His Move

Ricky was taking a spelling test when he saw the little spaceship return with three enormous Mecha-Monkeys.

45

"Hey," cried Ricky, "where's my Robot?"

"He got into a tight squeeze," laughed Major Monkey. "And he's never coming BACK – haw-haw-haw!"

"NOOOOO!" cried Ricky. But there was nothing he could do.

Major Monkey flew through the streets of Squeakyville and ordered everyone on Earth to surrender.

CHAPTER 7

The Mouse from SASA

That afternoon, Ricky sat in his bedroom missing his best friend.

"We are sure that your Robot will be OK," said Ricky's mother.

"Yes," said Ricky's father. "He'll find a way to escape. I just know it."

Soon, there was a knock on the front door. It was a general from the Squeakyville Air and Space Association.

"We are going to send a space shuttle up to Mars to rescue your mighty Robot," said the general. "He is our only hope."

"Hooray!" cried Ricky.

"And we need you to come
with us, Ricky," said the general.
"You know that Robot better
than anybody."

"Can I go?" Ricky asked his
parents. "Pleeeeease?"

"Well," said Ricky's father,
"all right. But you must
promise to be careful!"
"Hooray!" cried Ricky.

CHAPTER 8

The Space Shuttle

Ricky and his parents got into the general's car. The general turned on the rocket boosters, and they all flew straight to the Space Centre.

"This is *so cool*!" said Ricky's father.

Soon, Ricky was sitting
inside a giant space shuttle
with three real astro-mice.

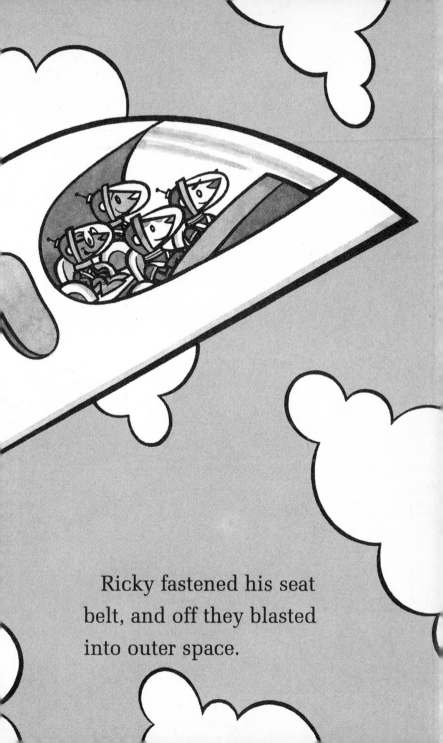

Ricky fastened his seat
belt, and off they blasted
into outer space.

When the shuttle arrived on
Mars, Ricky and the astro-mice
saw Major Monkey's laboratory.

They saw the mighty Robot
trapped inside the giant metal
hand. But what could they do?

Suddenly, another giant metal hand reached out of the hillside and grabbed the space shuttle.

61

Then the strange laboratory
began to rise from the ground.

It rose higher and higher . . .

. . . until finally it stepped out of the ground. Major Monkey's laboratory had turned into a colossal Orangu-Tron.

The astro-mice inside the space shuttle tried to open the emergency exit door, but it was stuck. It could only open halfway.

"I think I can fit through," said Ricky.

Ricky squeezed his way out of the space shuttle and headed towards the laboratory.

CHAPTER 9

Ricky to the Rescue

The Orangu-Tron stomped its feet as Ricky bravely climbed up its giant arm.

Soon, Ricky found a doorway
in the Orangu-Tron's ear, and he
crawled inside the strange laboratory.

Once inside, Ricky looked around
the control centre. He saw lots of evil
Robots and many strange machines.

69

Then, Ricky found the main power switch.

Ricky grabbed the switch and tried to turn off the power, but the switch was stuck. Ricky pulled and pulled on the switch.

ORANGU-TRON MAIN POWER SWITCH

Finally, Ricky was spotted by
an evil Robo-Chimp.

"Destroy the intruder!" said the
Robo-Chimp. "Destroy the
intruder!"

The Robo-Chimp grabbed Ricky's
breathing tube and started pulling.
Soon, other Robo-Chimps joined
in. Harder and harder they pulled.

Then Ricky had an idea. He wrapped his breathing tube around the main power switch and held on tight. The Robo-Chimps pulled and pulled. Finally, the switch began to move.

The harder the Robo-Chimps
pulled, the more the switch moved.
Ka-KLANK!
Suddenly, the power for the
whole laboratory turned off.
"Hooray!" cried Ricky.

CHAPTER 10

Freedom

Outside, the Orangu-Tron lost all of its power. Ricky's mighty Robot pushed his way out of the giant metal hand. He was free at last!

But inside, Ricky was in trouble. The Robo-Chimps rushed towards Ricky. "Must destroy intruder!" they chanted. "Must restore power!"

"HELP ME!" screamed Ricky
as the Robo-Chimps came
closer and closer.

KER-POW!
Ricky's Mighty Robot
punched a hole in the roof and
grabbed Ricky just in time.

78

Ricky pushed the SELF-DESTRUCT button with his tail. "Let's get out of here!" cried Ricky as the laboratory began to shake and crumble.

With Ricky in one hand and the
space shuttle in the other, Ricky's
Mighty Robot zoomed into space —
just in time.

KA-BOOOOOOOOM!

"That takes care of Mars," said Ricky. "Now we have to save Earth!"

CHAPTER 11

Back to Earth

When they got back to Earth, Ricky's mighty Robot spotted Major Monkey.

"What-what are *YOU* doing here?" asked Major Monkey.

"We're here to save Earth!" said Ricky.

83

"Oh, yeah?" said Major Monkey. "We'll see about that!" He called his Mecha-Monkeys and ordered them to destroy Ricky's mighty Robot.

Ricky's Robot put Ricky and
the space shuttle somewhere safe.
Then the robo-battle began.

Ricky's Robot treated
the Mecha-Monkeys to
two servings of *punch* . . .

... one *karate chop* ...

. . . and a *knuckle sandwich*.

Major Monkey was very upset.
"All right, banana brains," he
shouted. "Quit monkeying
around! Let's see some action!"

CHAPTER 12

The Big Battle

(IN FLIP-O-RAMA™)

O-RaMa
HERE'S HOW IT WORKS!

STEP 1
Place your *left* hand inside the dotted lines marked "LEFT HAND HERE". Hold the book open *flat*.

STEP 2
Grasp the *right-hand* page with your right thumb and index finger (inside the dotted lines marked "RIGHT THUMB HERE").

STEP 3
Now *quickly* flip the right-hand page back and forth until the picture appears to be *animated*.

(For extra fun, try adding your own sound effects!)

FLIP-O-RAMA 1

(pages 97 and 99)

Remember, flip *only* page 97.
While you are flipping, make sure
you can see the picture on page 97
and the one on page 99.
If you flip quickly, the two
pictures will start to look like
<u>one</u> *animated* picture.

Don't forget to add
your own sound effects!

LEFT HAND HERE

The Mecha-Monkeys Attacked.

RIGHT
THUMB
HERE

The Mecha-Monkeys Attacked.

FLIP-O-RAMA 2

(pages 101 and 103)

Remember, flip *only* page 101.
While you are flipping, make sure
you can see the picture on page 101
and the one on page 103.
If you flip quickly, the two
pictures will start to look like
<u>one</u> *animated* picture.

Don't forget to add
your own sound effects!

LEFT HAND HERE

Ricky's Robot
Fought Back.

101

RIGHT
THUMB
HERE

102

Ricky's Robot
Fought Back.

FLIP-O-RAMA 3

(pages 105 and 107)

Remember, flip *only* page 105.
While you are flipping, make sure
you can see the picture on page 105
and the one on page 107.
If you flip quickly, the two
pictures will start to look like
<u>one</u> *animated* picture.

Don't forget to add
your own sound effects!

LEFT HAND HERE

The Mecha-Monkeys Battled Hard.

RIGHT
THUMB
HERE

The Mecha-Monkeys Battled Hard.

FLIP-O-RAMA 4

(pages 109 and 111)

Remember, flip *only* page 109.
While you are flipping, make sure
you can see the picture on page 109
and the one on page 111.
If you flip quickly, the two
pictures will start to look like
<u>one</u> *animated* picture.

Don't forget to add
your own sound effects!

LEFT HAND HERE

Ricky's Robot
Battled Harder.

109

Ricky's Robot
Battled Harder.

FLIP-O-RAMA 5

(pages 113 and 115)

Remember, flip *only* page 113.
While you are flipping, make sure
you can see the picture on page 113
and the one on page 115.
If you flip quickly, the two
pictures will start to look like
<u>one</u> *animated* picture.

Don't forget to add
your own sound effects!

LEFT HAND HERE

Ricky's Robot
Won the War.

RIGHT THUMB HERE

114

Ricky's Robot
Won the War.

CHAPTER 13

Paying for Mistakes

Poor Major Monkey. His Mecha-Monkeys flew home to Mars, and he could not rule the world any more.

"Boo-hoo-hoo!" cried Major
Monkey. "I've made a big mistake."

"Yes," said Ricky. "And now you
must pay for your mistake!"

Together, the two heroes put
Major Monkey where he belonged:
in the Squeakyville prison.

"Thank you boys for saving Earth," said the general. "If there's anything we can do to repay you, please let me know!"

Ricky whispered in
his Robot's ear. The Robot
nodded his giant head.

"Well, sir," said Ricky, "we sure
could use a new people carrier."

"All right," said the general.
"How many would you like?"

CHAPTER 14

Heroes

Ricky and his mighty Robot flew
back to the Space Centre to meet
Ricky's parents.

"Mum! Dad!" cried Ricky.
"Look what the general gave us.
A brand-new people carrier!"

"Wow!" said Ricky's mother.
"We'll race you home!" said
Ricky's father.

So Ricky Ricotta and his mighty Robot raced the rocket-powered people carrier all the way home.

Soon, the whole Ricotta family
was safe at home eating cheese
pizza and drinking lemonade.

"Thank you for rescuing each
other today," said Ricky's mother.

"Yes," said Ricky's father,
"and thank you for paying for
your mistake."

"No problem," said Ricky.

127

"That's what friends are for!"

HOW TO DRAW RICKY

1.

2.

3.

4.

5.

6.

7.

8.

9.

10.

11.

12.

HOW TO DRAW RICKY'S ROBOT

1.

2.

3.

4.

5.

6.

HOW TO DRAW MAJOR MONKEY

1.

2.

3.

4.

5.

6.

7.

8.

9.

10.

11.

12.

HOW TO DRAW A MECHA-MONKEY

1.

2.

3.

4.

5.

6.

7.

8.

9.

10.

11.

12.

HOW TO DRAW AN ORANGU-TRON

1.

2.

3.

4.

5.

6.

HOW TO DRAW A ROBO-CHIMP

1.

2.

3.

4.

5.

6.

7.

8.

9.

10.

11.

12.

COMING SOON:

Ricky Ricotta's Mighty Robot

vs

The Jurassic Jack Rabbits from Jupiter

The Stupid Stinkbugs from Saturn

The Uranium Unicorns from Uranus

The Naughty Night Crawlers from Neptune

The Un-Pleasant Penguins from Pluto

About the Author and Illustrator

DAV PILKEY created his first stories as comic books while he was in elementary school. In 1997, he wrote and illustrated his first adventure novel for children, *The Adventures of Captain Underpants*, which received rave reviews and was an instant best-seller — as were the other books that followed in the series. Dav is also the creator of numerous award-winning picture books. He and his dog live in Seattle, Washington.

It was a stroke of luck when Dav discovered the work of artist **MARTIN ONTIVEROS**. Dav knew that Martin was just the right illustrator for the Ricky Ricotta's Mighty Robot series. Martin lives in Portland, Oregon. He has a lot of toys as well as two cats, Bunny and Spanky.

> Visit Dav Pilkey's Extra-Crunchy
> Web Site O'Fun at:
> www.pilkey.com